The
GREAT GETAWAY

To the real Jennifer and Elizabeth and the
rest of the Whiteley family — my friends.
Olga

For Ilze, Ian, and Esther with love.
Ellen

For a free color catalog describing Gareth Stevens' list of
high-quality children's books, call 1-800-341-3569 (USA)
or 1-800-461-9120 (Canada).

Library of Congress Cataloging-in-Publication Data

Cossi, Olga.
    The great getaway / by Olga Cossi.
      p.   cm.
    Summary: Two young sisters decide that while running away can be
adventurous it is much more fun to come home.
    ISBN 0-8368-0107-5
    [1. Sisters—Fiction. 2. Runaways—Fiction.] I. Title.
PZ7.C819Gr   1991
[E]—dc20   89-42637

First published in the United States and Canada in 1991 by
Gareth Stevens Children's Books
1555 North RiverCenter Drive, Suite 201
Milwaukee, Wisconsin 53212, USA

Text copyright © 1991 by Olga Cossi
Illustrations copyright © 1991 by Ellen Anderson
Format copyright © 1991 by Gareth Stevens, Inc.

Printed in the United States of America

1 2 3 4 5 6 7 8 9 97 96 95 94 93 92 91

The
GREAT GETAWAY

by Olga Cossi • illustrated by Ellen Anderson

Gareth Stevens Children's Books
MILWAUKEE

First it was the twins. Ever since they were born, Mom and Dad were always busy, busy, busy.

Then for lunch that day, Elizabeth and Jennifer found on each plate a nest of the nastiest, fattest cooked green beans they had ever seen.

That did it!

"Let's run away," whispered Elizabeth. "No more twins. No more green beans!"

"Right," said Jennifer.

Big sisters are always right.

So Elizabeth and Jennifer hurried to their room. They filled their suitcases with all the toys they just had to take with them.

When the suitcases were full, there were a lot of favorite toys left over.

"Let's put these toys in the big laundry basket," Elizabeth said. "We can take them, too."

"Right," said Jennifer.

So they filled the laundry basket with toys. And they strapped their skates to the bottom of the basket so it would roll.

Then they carried their suitcases and pushed the laundry basket past the bathroom where Mom and Dad were busy bathing the twins.

They rolled out the front door and out the iron gate that led to the sidewalk.

"I think we should go this way," said Elizabeth.

"Right," said Jennifer.

So the two sisters hurried along, carrying their suitcases and pushing the laundry basket full of toys between them.

The wheels of the skates sang a song as they rolled over the cracks in the sidewalk.

"Clickety-clack! Clickety-clack!
We're running away,
and we'll never come back!"

When they got to the corner, Elizabeth and Jennifer stopped. They had never before crossed the street **alone!**

"Let's turn the corner and walk one more block," said Elizabeth.
Jennifer nodded. Elizabeth was right.
This time, the skate wheels sang,

"Clickety-clack! Clickety-clack!
We made it this far,
and we're not going back."

Soon Elizabeth and Jennifer got tired. They sat on the sidewalk and played with their toys while they rested.

Then they were on their way again. Now the wheels sang merrily,

"Clackety-click! Clackety-click!
The twins are boring,
and green beans are sick!"

At the next corner, Elizabeth said, "This looks like a good place to cross the street. Come on, Jennifer."

Very carefully, they rolled the laundry basket over the curb.

Just then, a red sports car zo-o-oomed by! Then a station wagon and a huge truck. Zo-o-o-oom! Zoo-o-oo-oom!

Elizabeth and Jennifer scrambled back onto the sidewalk.

"This is **not** a safe place to cross the street!" decided Elizabeth. "We'll walk down one more block."

Elizabeth was right again.

They turned the corner. Jennifer reached for Elizabeth's hand while the skate wheels sang a brave new song.

"Clickety-clack! Clickety-clack!
Nothing can scare us
or make us go back."

At the next corner, Elizabeth said, "I'm sure we can cross here."

They stepped down from the curb.
Two shiny black motorcycles roared
around the corner and thundered by.
Hastily, Elizabeth and Jennifer
scrambled back onto the sidewalk.

"That was close!" gulped Elizabeth.
"Right!" agreed Jennifer.

They walked on.

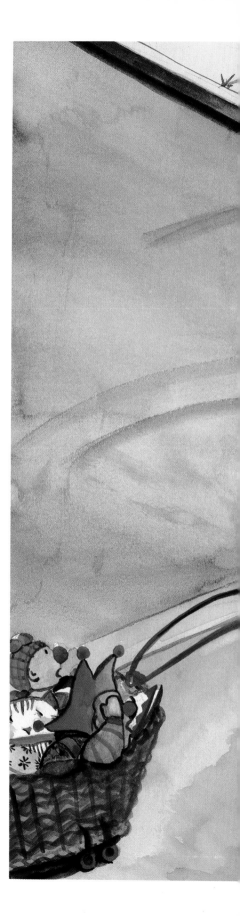

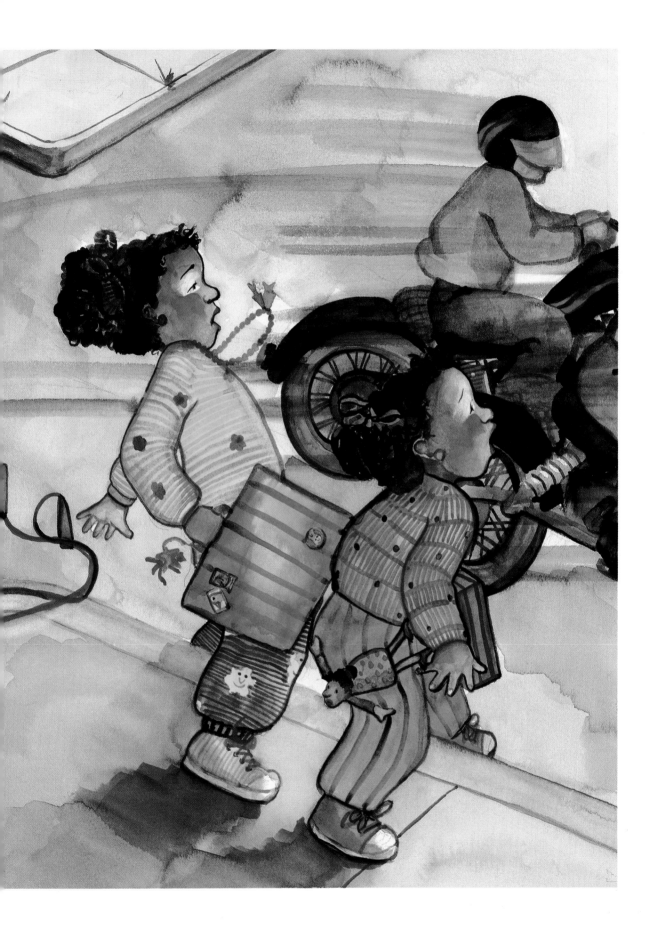

By the time the two sisters reached the fourth corner, the skate wheels were singing another song.

"Clickety-clack. Clickety-clack.
Are we still having fun,
or should we go back?"

"We'd better cross the street this time," Elizabeth warned.

They looked both ways, twice. Then they started to cross.

All of a sudden, a huge, shaggy dog came bounding toward them from across the street.

"Wroof! Wroof! Wroof!" he barked, his ears flopping and his long tongue hanging out.

"Oh, oh! Let's run!" Elizabeth shouted.

They pulled the laundry basket back up on the sidewalk, rolled around the corner, and raced down the block as fast as they could go!

By then the skate wheels were singing a different song.

"Clickety-clack! Clickety-clack!
We'll be ever so happy
if we just make it back!"

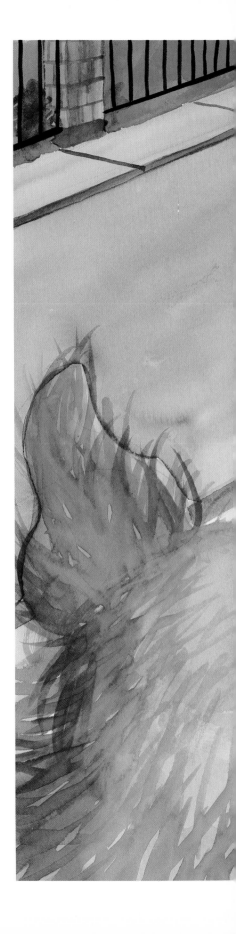

The dog was catching up when Elizabeth saw a familiar iron gate. It was theirs! She pushed it open and ran inside, pulling Jennifer and their toys with her. The gate slammed shut behind them before the dog could squeeze through.

"Look, we're home!" cried Elizabeth. "We only ran around the block!"
"You're right!" sighed Jennifer.

They rolled the laundry basket into the house.

They rolled it past the bathroom where Mom and Dad were still busy with the twins.

And they rolled it to their room.

They put away their toys,
 the suitcases,
 the skates,
 and the laundry basket.

Then they hurried to the kitchen. They were hungry!

"Running away was fun, wasn't it?" Elizabeth whispered as they sat in the kitchen, eating cold cooked green beans and drinking milk.

"Yes," agreed Jennifer. "But so is coming home!"

Elizabeth nodded. This time, it was Jennifer's turn to be right!